This book belongs to:

_____

Introduction

It's *Rindin the Puffer*™. He's an odd-looking fish with googly eyes and no chin! He has big buckteeth in his ridiculous grin, but what makes him different and unique most of all… is when he's frightened, he expands like a prickly beach ball!

Our story begins with Rindin being the target of a joke, just for being different. However, when the bullies meet up with a hungry barracuda, Rindin saves the day!

Rindin the Puffer™ shows the importance of 'being yourself' while respecting individual differences in others.

CNW Entertainment presents *Rindin the Puffer*™, the first story in the CrocPond™ family of products, and the award-winning DVD that is included with this book. Rindin inspires children of all ages to be more tolerant, helping them to see their peers in a positive new light.

Our vision for the CrocPond™ family of products is to make a difference in the lives of children of all cultures. Our products are the tools that assist children along with their parents, teachers and caregivers to inspire wise choices in life while encouraging others to do the same.

Created and book adaptation by
Roger Anthony

Based on original story by
Len Simon

Edited by
David Farland

Illustrations by
FatCat Animation Studios

This book is dedicated to Aaron, Alexander, Anya Paige, Conner, Cooper, Donna, Jared, Jessica, Jordan, Mia, Nadine, Natalie, Nicole, Patricia, Patrick, Pernilla, Sean, Skyler, Stanton, Vanessa and all the children of the world.

Library of Congress Cataloging-in-Publication Data
CNW Entertainment
   Rindin the Puffer™ / CNW Entertainment
      p. cm.
   Summary: Our story begins with Rindin being the target of a joke, just for being different. However, when the bullies meet up with a hungry barracuda, Rindin saves the day!
   ISBN 0-9798297-0-4 (Rindin the Puffer™ DVD bonus set (hardcover))
   ISBN 978-0-9798297-0-3

With special thanks to Inland Graphics, Menomonee Falls, Wisconsin 83051

10   9   8   7   6   5   4   3   2   1

the

PUFFER

by

Just like people,
like you and me,
fish come in all shapes
and colors
under the sea.

Some are big. Some are small.

Some are the size of a shopping mall.

But among them all, one fish is

unlike any other...

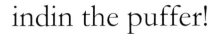 indin the puffer!

He's an odd-looking fish with googly eyes and no chin. He has big buckteeth in his ridiculous grin, but what makes him different and unique most of all... is when he's frightened, he expands like a prickly beach ball!

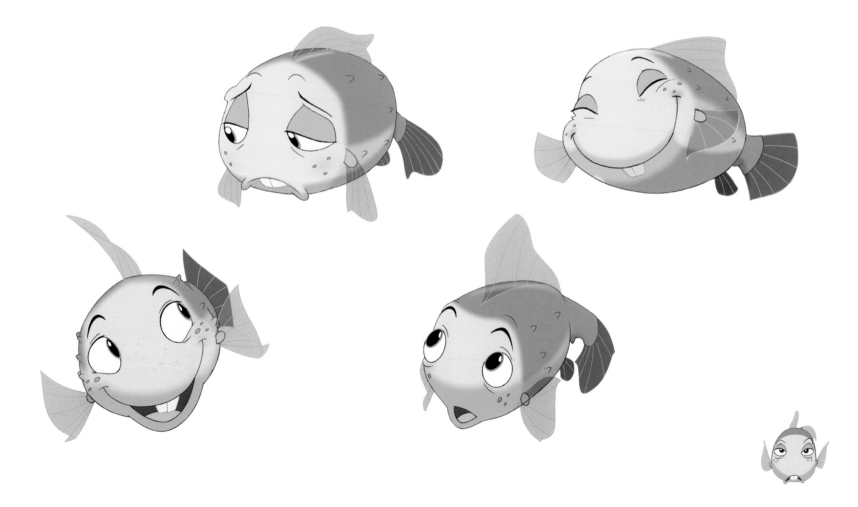

One day Rindin went searching for someone to play with.

Lenny, Bo and Shimmer were hanging around a coral reef when they noticed Rindin swimming toward them. "Here comes that weirdo Rindin," said Bo. "Let's play a joke on him!"

They quickly hid. As Rindin neared, they lunged out and surprised him. Rindin got such a shock that he puffed up in fright. Lenny, Bo and Shimmer laughed as they swam away.

indin wondered sadly, *why am I so different from other fish?*

Soon a pretty young seahorse came along. "Hi!" said Rindin. Startled, the seahorse squirted off fast as a squid. Rindin followed. Swimming around a corner, Rindin bumped into a shiny bottle.

"Yikes!" he yelled, puffing up at his own twisted reflection. Rindin calmed down and returned to his normal size. He

thought, *puffing up makes it so hard to make friends.* Again, Rindin was alone and sad. But he put a smile on, determined to find someone to play with.

earby, Lenny, Bo and Shimmer were looking for something fun to do. Lenny noticed an old wreck off in the distance.

"Hey guys, look over there!" he said. The others came to see what he was fussing about.

"What's that?" asked Bo.

Lenny responded, "Let's go and check it out!"

Shimmer gulped, "I don't know. We're not supposed to stray too far from the reef."

"Come on," said Bo. "Don't be a spoilsport."

Not wanting to disappoint her friends, Shimmer hesitantly followed.

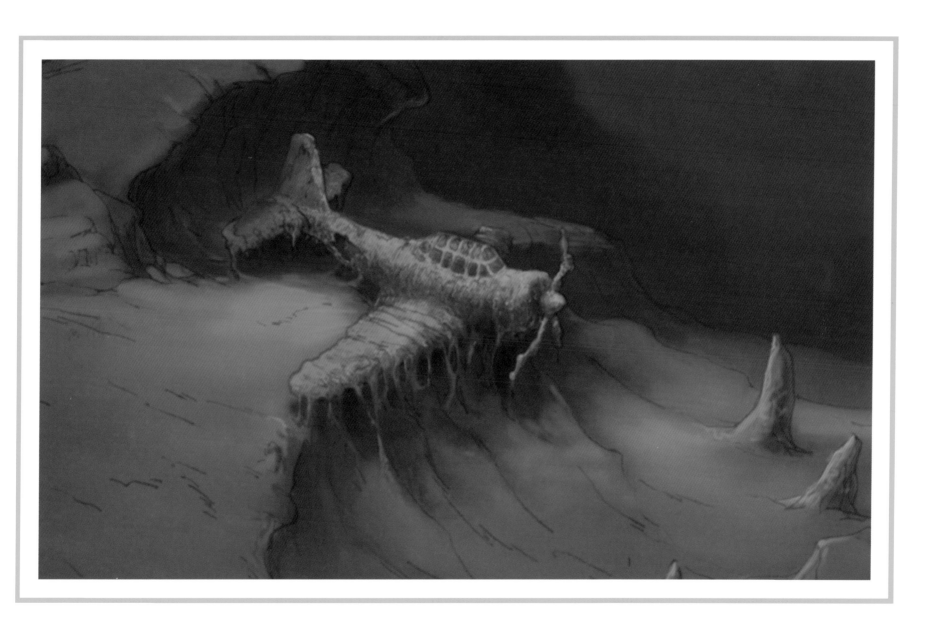

Soon they were swimming where they shouldn't. They were having so much fun that they didn't notice a shadow silently following their every move.

"Something is wrong," whispered Shimmer, "I'm getting chills up my scales."

"You're imagining things," said Bo.

"Oh no!" Shimmer yelped. "It's a barracuda!"

All three were scared right out of their fins! They took off in terror, with the barracuda close behind. They zigged and zagged trying to lose the big fish, but he kept on coming.

himmer knew that they couldn't keep this up for long. Spotting a narrow opening in the window of the plane, she cried, "In here!"

Lenny darted in, Bo followed.

"Oomph! I'm stuck!" shouted Bo. He was too plump to fit through the window.

"Lenny, help!" cried Shimmer. "Quickly! The barracuda's coming!"

With all their might, Lenny pulled as Shimmer pushed. The barracuda lunged. Its cruel jaws snapped shut just as Bo and Shimmer popped into the wreck.

"ikes, that was close!" cried Bo.

"Waaay too close!" said Shimmer.

Lenny shouted, "He's coming back!"

The barracuda charged. CRASH! The plane shuddered as the barracuda slammed into it.

Unable to break in, the barracuda glared at the three young fish and then considered his next move as he glided off into the shadows.

eanwhile, nearby, Rindin met a hermit crab. "Will you play with me?" he asked.

The timid crab fled into his shell.

Rejected again, Rindin shrugged off his sadness and continued on.

Back at the wreck, Lenny said, "I think the barracuda's gone. Let's make a run for it!" Cautiously the young fish crept out of the wreck.

From a distance, Rindin spotted the young fish. *Oh, a game of hide-and-seek!* he thought. "That looks fun!"

"ou should have seen the look on your faces!" laughed Lenny, trying to sound brave as he swam from the plane.

Shimmer whispered, "Shhhh! The barracuda could still be nearby."

The three bolted from rock to rock, trying to keep out of sight from the barracuda.

Suddenly, the barracuda swam out of hiding, blocking their path.

"Oh no!" cried Shimmer.

Lightning fast, the three raced into a cave! Unfortunately, they came to a dead end.

ow I know the meaning of *dead end*," gulped Lenny. "We're dead, and this is the end!"

The barracuda licked his lips as he glided close.

Suddenly Rindin appeared. "Hi guys!"

He smiled at the three, unaware of the danger lurking behind him.

enny, Bo and Shimmer froze. At first, Rindin thought that *he* had frightened them, but he noticed they were staring past him. Rindin turned just as the barracuda's jaws snapped shut!

"Yikes!" the other fish shouted. "He ate Rindin!"

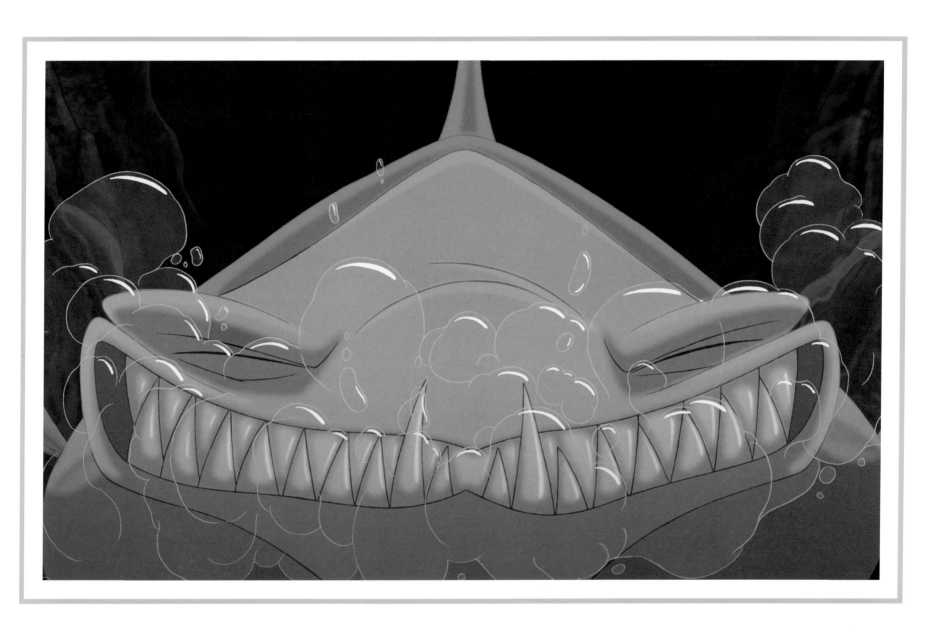

ut at that very second, everyone was startled by a loud CRACK! Rindin, doing what puffer fish do, puffed up, and the barracuda's jaw sprang open.

Rindin broke free!

The barracuda swam away with a sore jaw, confused and bewildered.

"ooray for Rindin!" Bo cried. "He's the bestest!"

"That was awesome!" said Lenny.

"Rindin, you saved us!" said Shimmer. "We're sorry we made fun of you."

Rindin's new friends tossed him up again and again in celebration.

"You're so cool!" said Bo. "Can you teach me how to puff up?"

At last I've made some friends, thought Rindin. *They accept me for who I am. I'm glad I'm not like any other fish in the sea! I'm really, really glad I'm ME!*

The End.

Fun Fish Facts

Puffer fish really do puff up when they are scared!
They inflate themselves by pumping water into their stomachs. Their predator ends up getting quite the mouthful.

Sharks don't get sick!
Their immune systems are so powerful that sharks do not suffer from any known disease. Doctors hope that by studying them, we can learn how to better treat illnesses in people.

Fish can talk!
By using special microphones, scientists have found that most fish communicate with each other by making soft clicks or squeals. Many fish can also communicate by changing colors (either to attract other fish or scare them away), and by posture. For example, by raising the spines on their backs, they warn other fish away.

The biggest fish in the sea is the Whale Shark!
Its mouth is wider than you are tall! It gets up to 46 feet long and weighs up to 15 tons.

The Climbing Perch sometimes climb trees!
It can stay out of the water for weeks at a time and has the ability to walk using its fins.

Acknowledgments

We are deeply grateful to everyone who has contributed to make this book possible especially Nicholas Zaldastani and Susan Atherton.

A special thanks to our business partners, associates, the Humane Society of the United States for their sponsorship and support, and the FatCat Studio crew who, in their hard work, determination, long hours, patience and dedication to their craft, were able to make the movie and the book possible.

We are particularly grateful to all our families for their unyielding love and support, especially considering the travel schedules and the demands of the production resulting in long hours away from home.

— CNW Entertainment

Final Note

The wonder and magic of *Rindin the Puffer*™ is in the intuitive experience people from all walks of life, be it children or adults, will feel from the story and characters. A special 'something' that takes hold and gives that 'aha!' moment. This moment empowers them to apply their own personal experience of *Rindin*™ to their lives where needed. This alone is beyond measure! Therein lies the wonder and magic of *Rindin the Puffer*™!

Other CrocPond™ stories coming soon: *Dex's Gym, Babysitting Bolper, Beehive Bootcamp*

For more information about the characters and stories in the CrocPond™ family of products, please visit www.crocpond.com.